This Book Belongs To:

_____

_____

Dear Parents,

This coloring book is designed for young children who love all things that go. Cars, planes, trucks, trains, and more!

What makes this coloring book different from others:

- Big simple pictures perfect for beginners
- Drawings designed so it's easy to stay inside the lines
- Thick outlines and large areas to color
- No movie or cartoon characters

Coloring is fun for kids and has lots of benefits including:

- Improves fine motor skills
- Prepares children for school
- Contributes to better handwriting
- Color awareness and recognition
- Improves focus and hand eye coordination

Hope your child likes this book!

We would love to hear from you. If you have feedback, please email us at feedback@littlephone.co

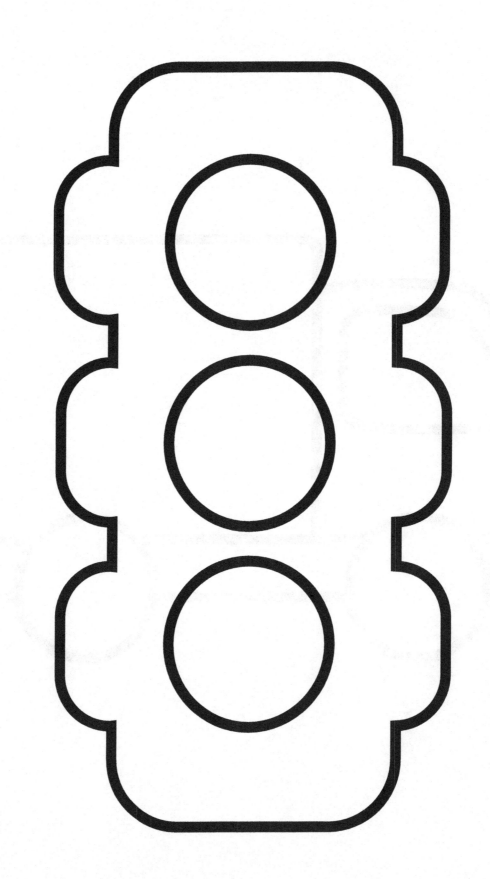

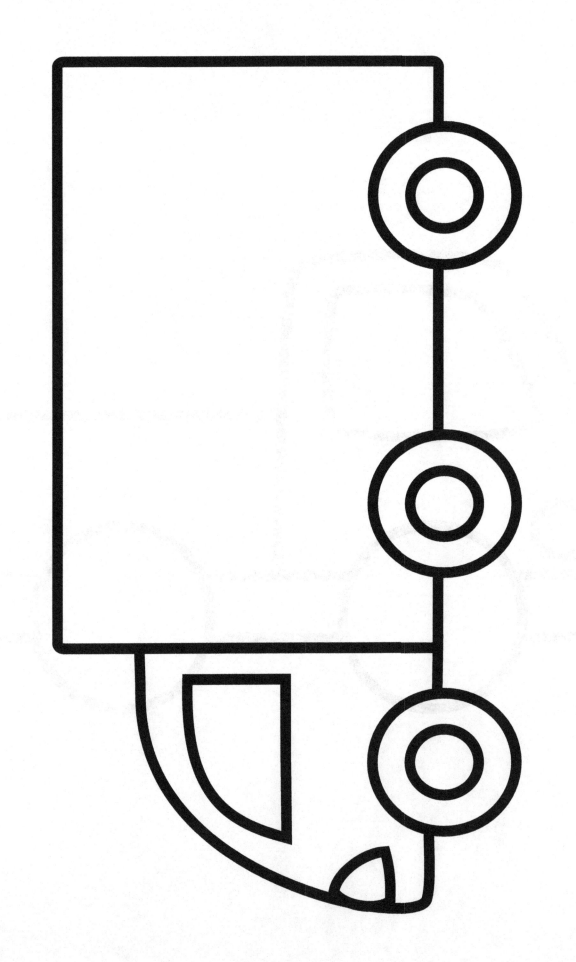

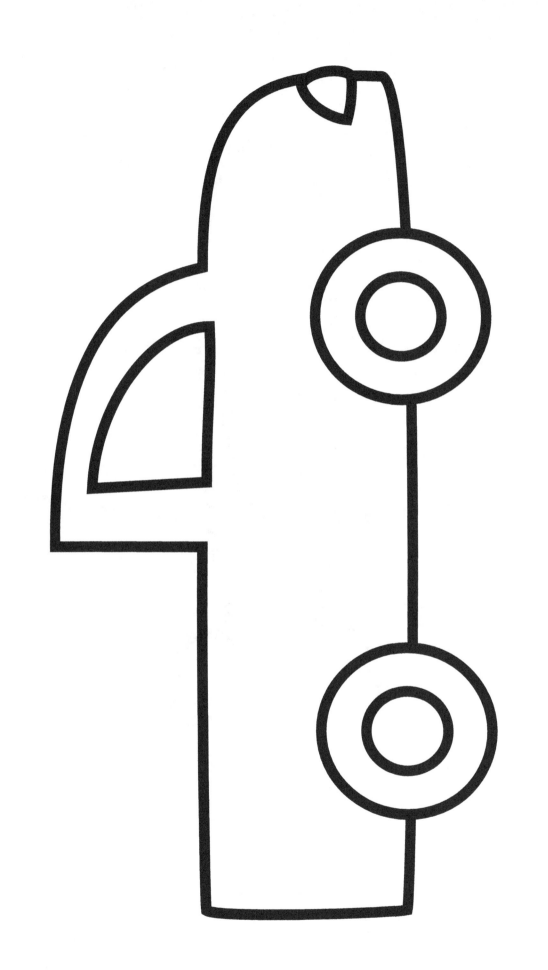

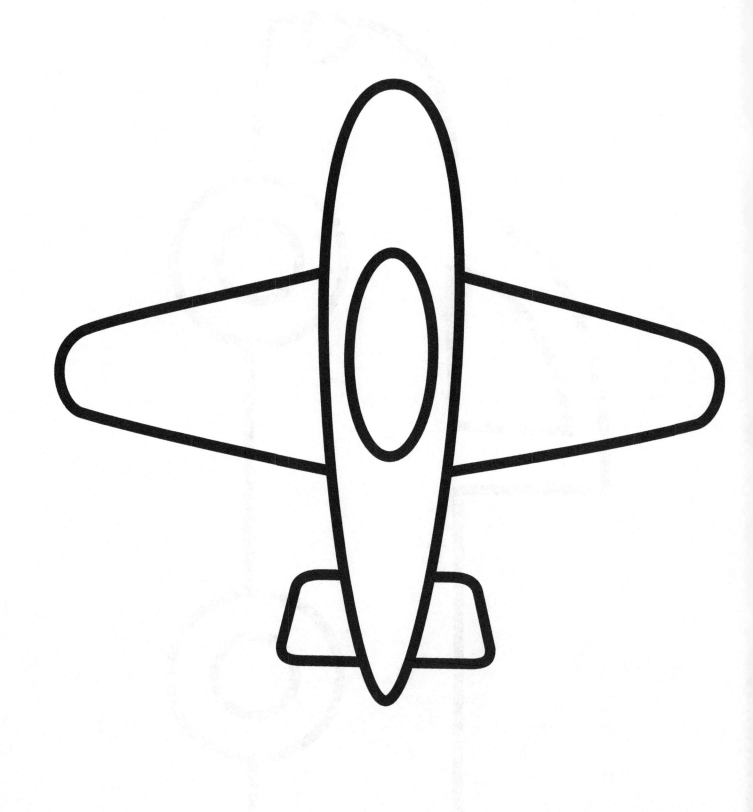

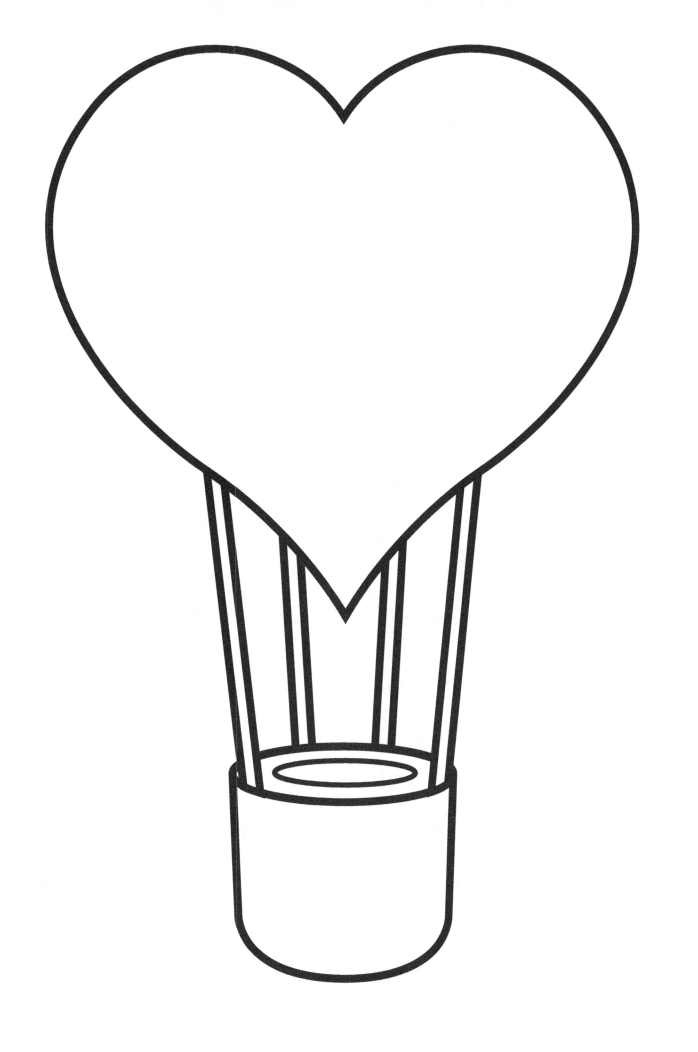

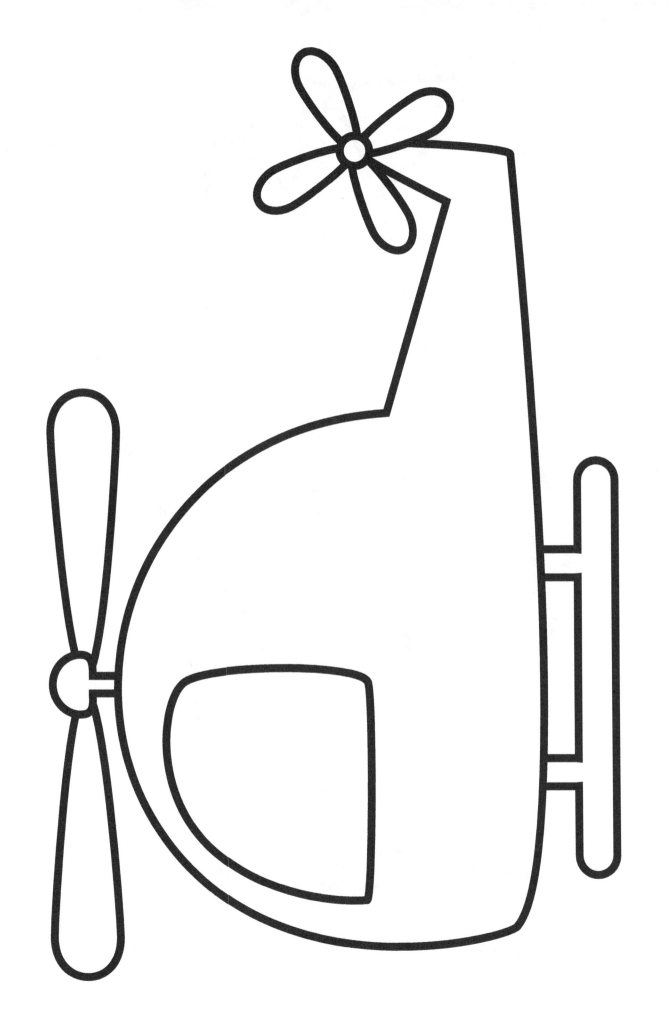

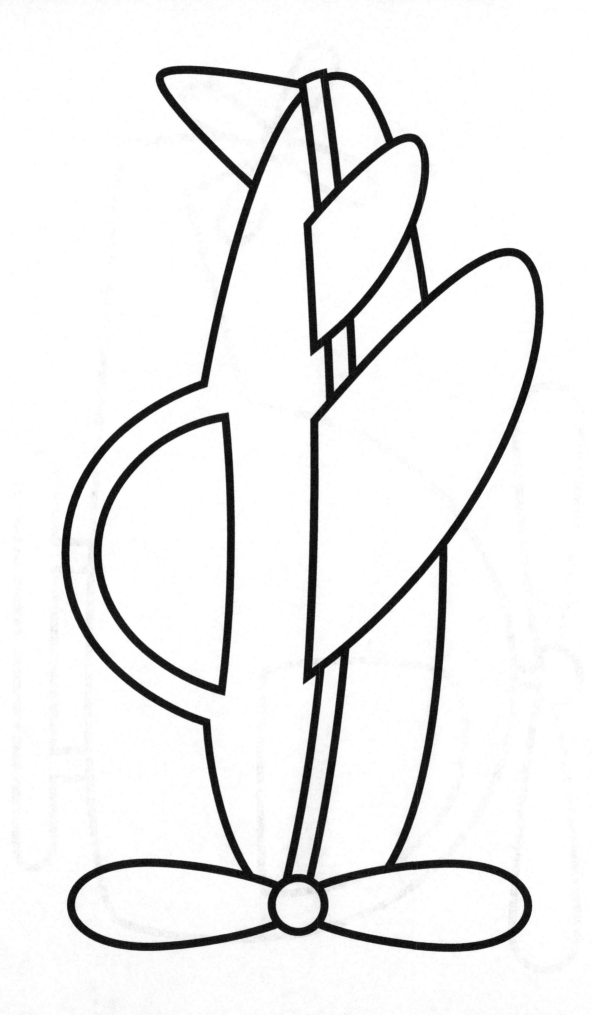

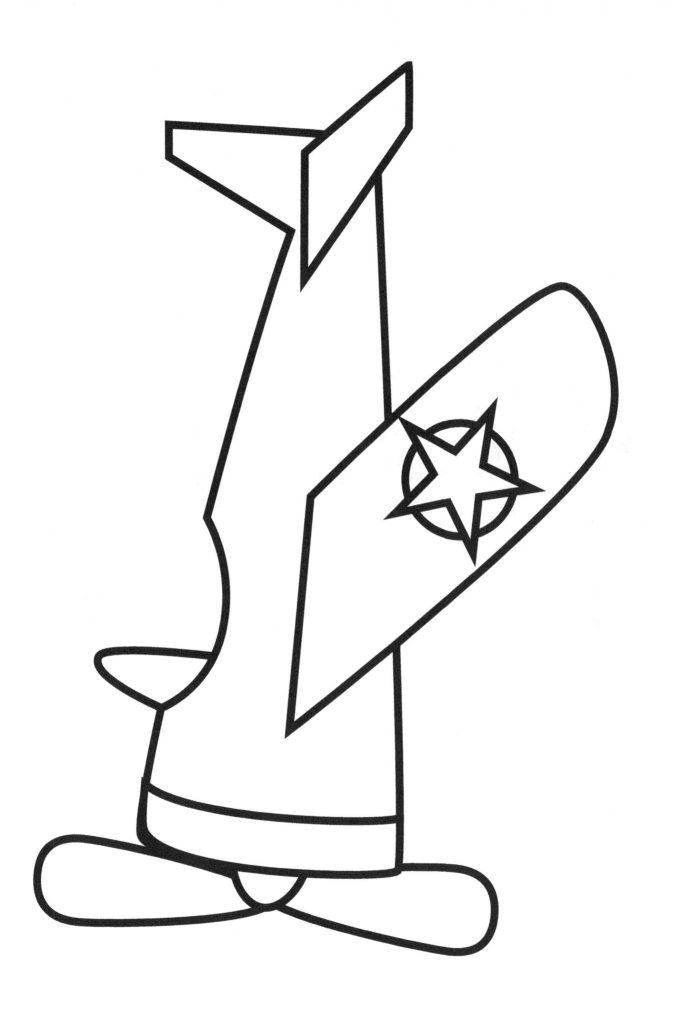

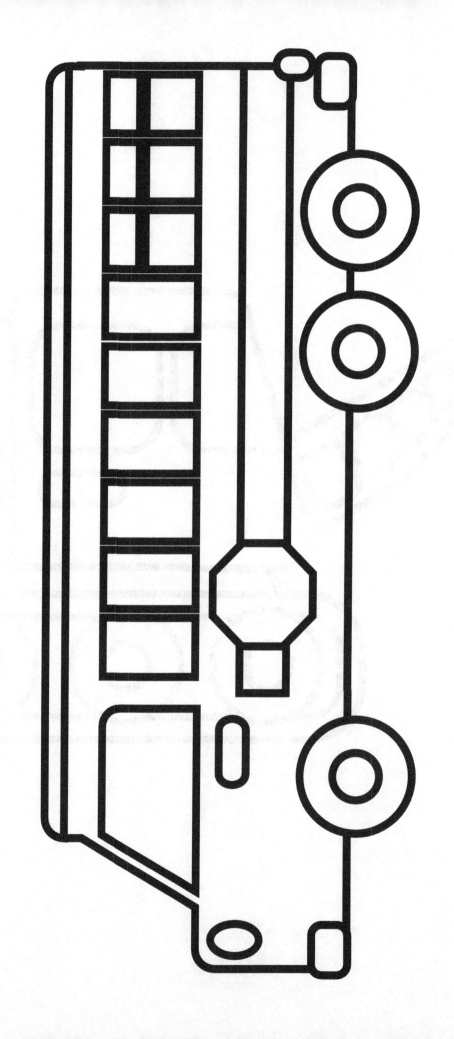

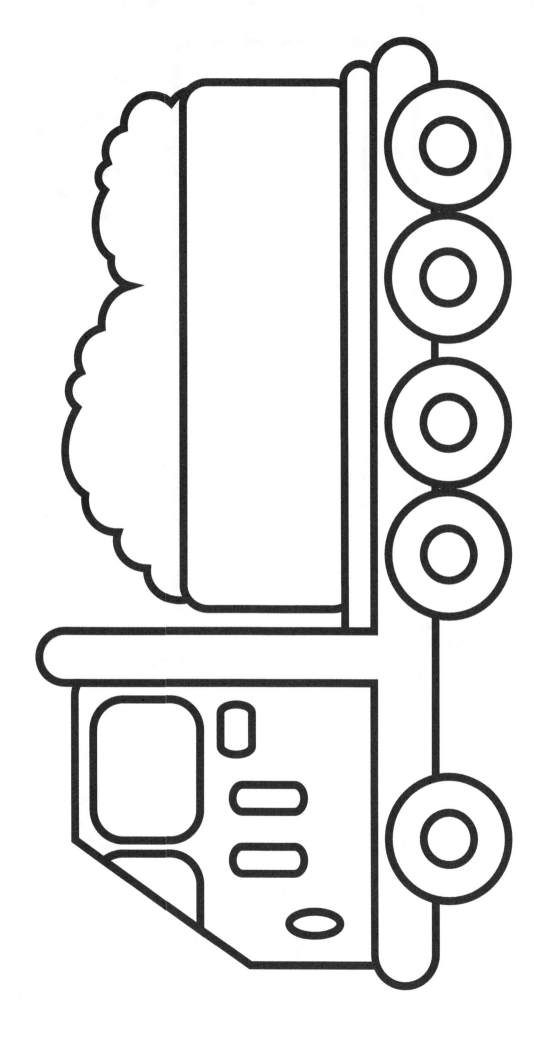

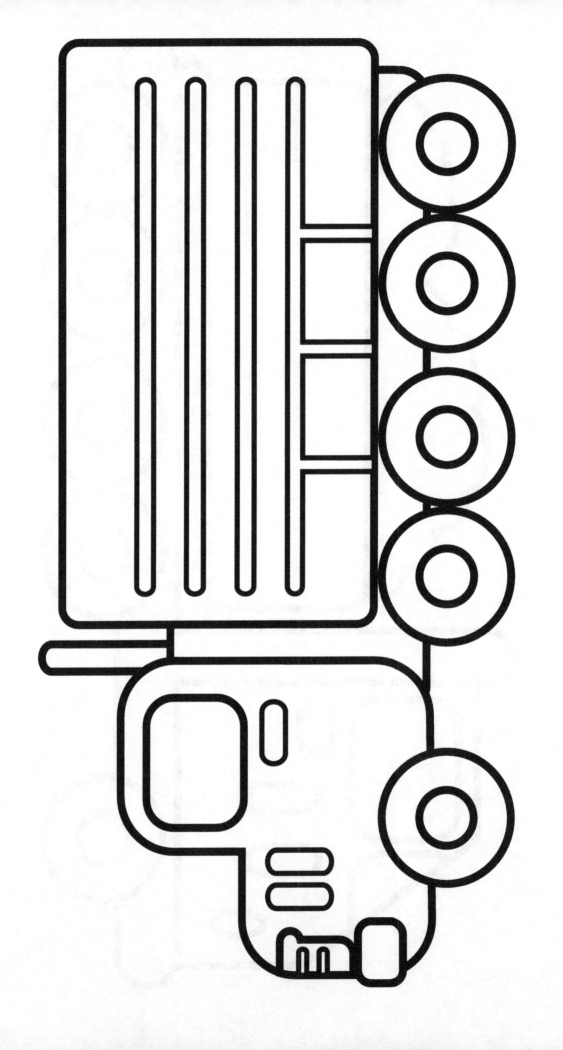

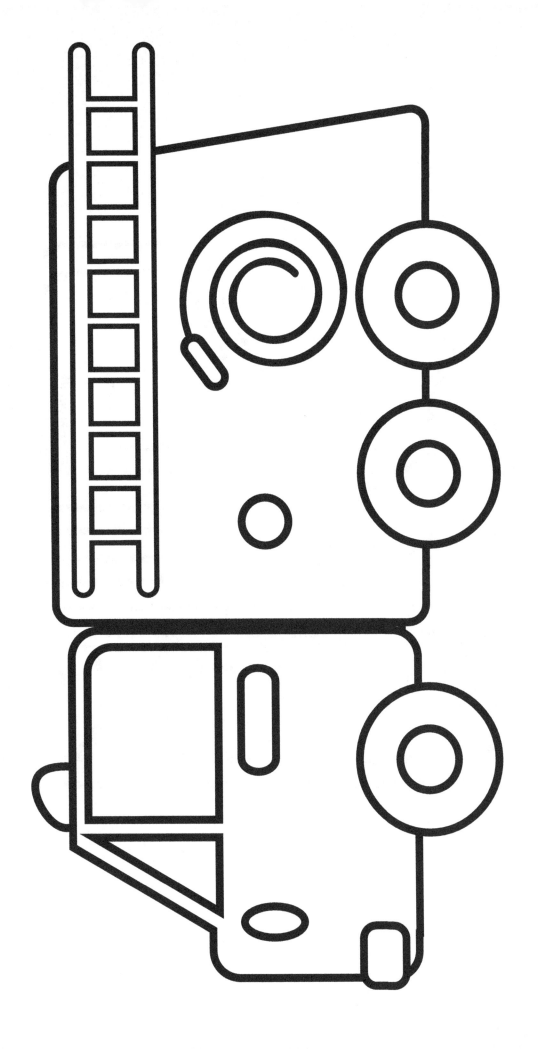

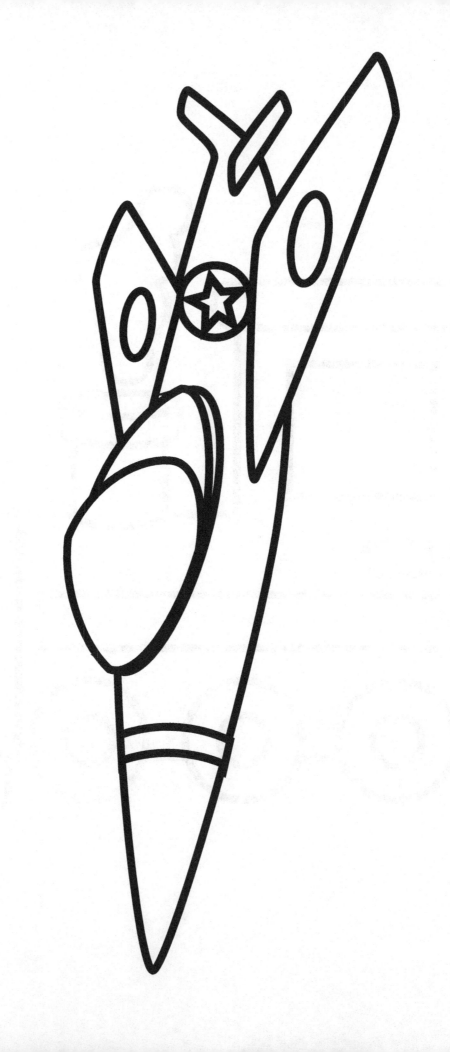

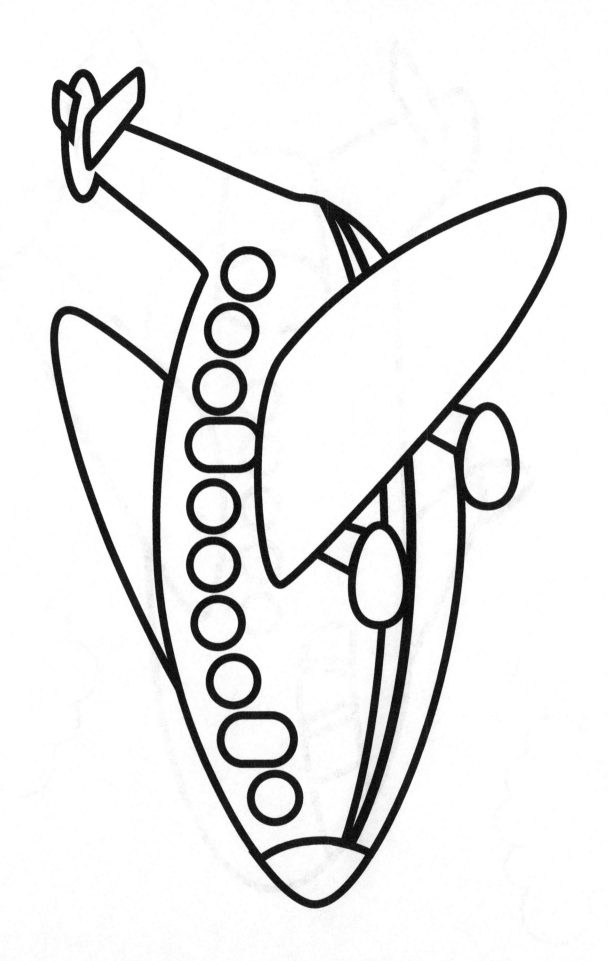

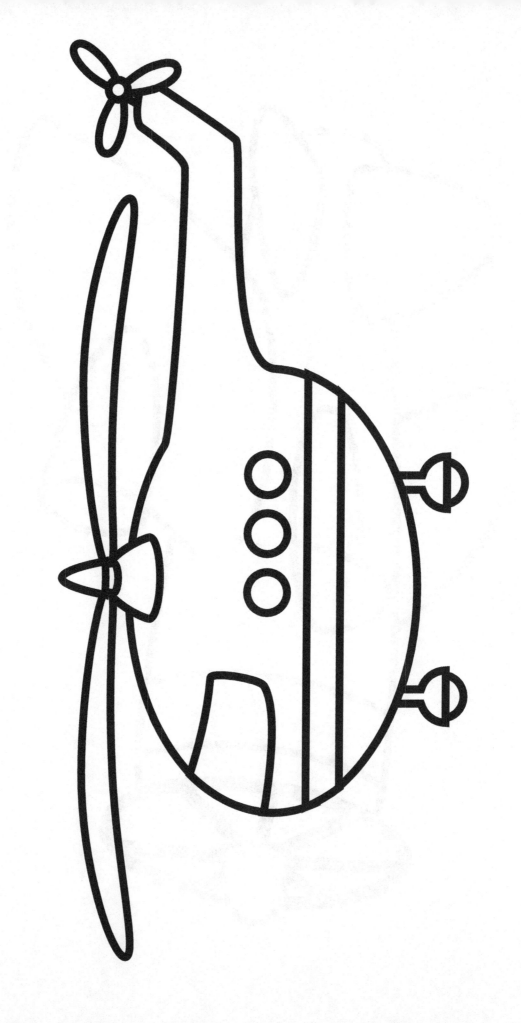

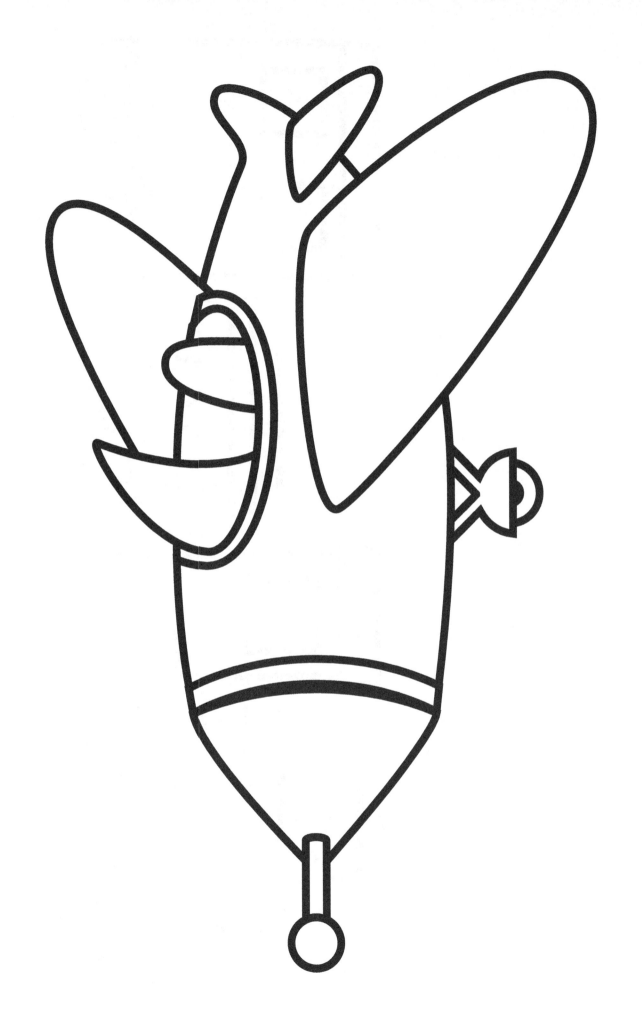

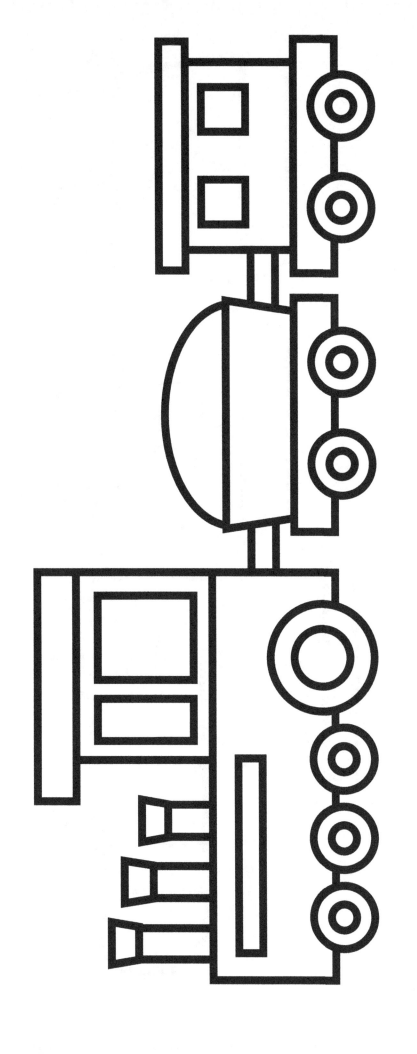

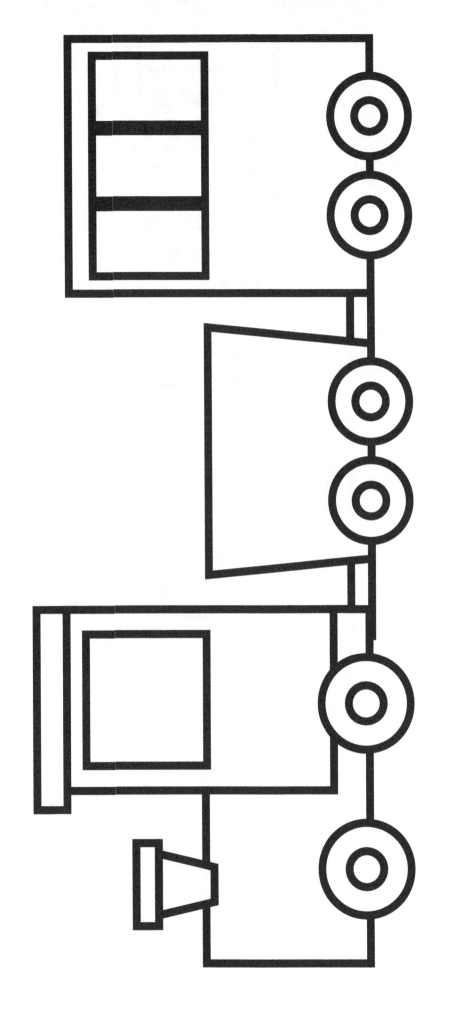

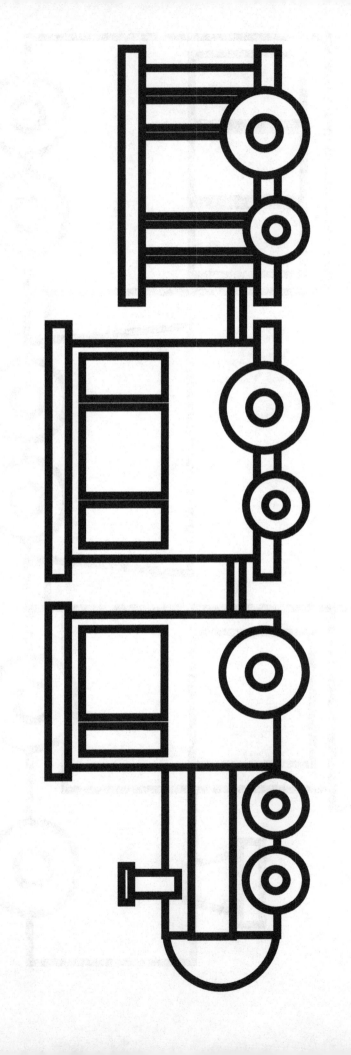

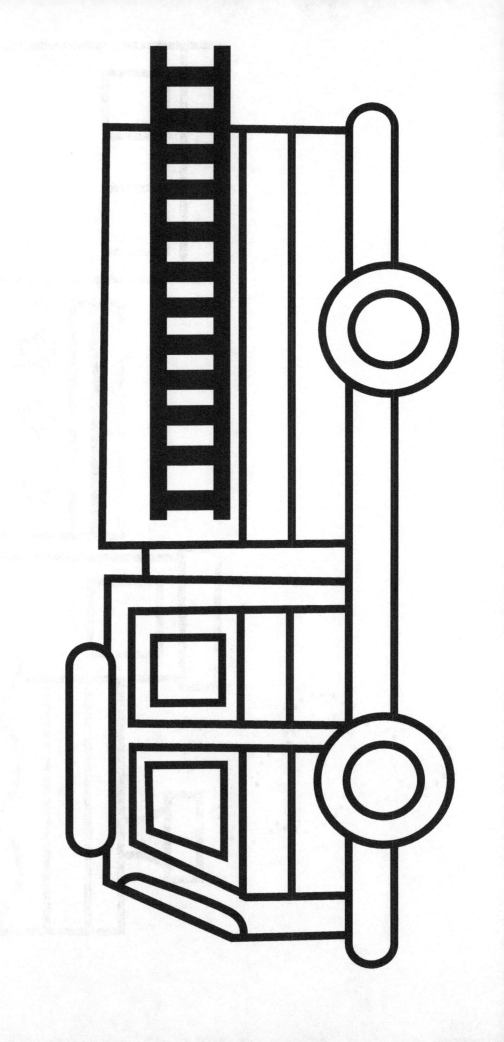

Great Job!

The next half of the book contains the same images as the first half so you can color your favorites again!

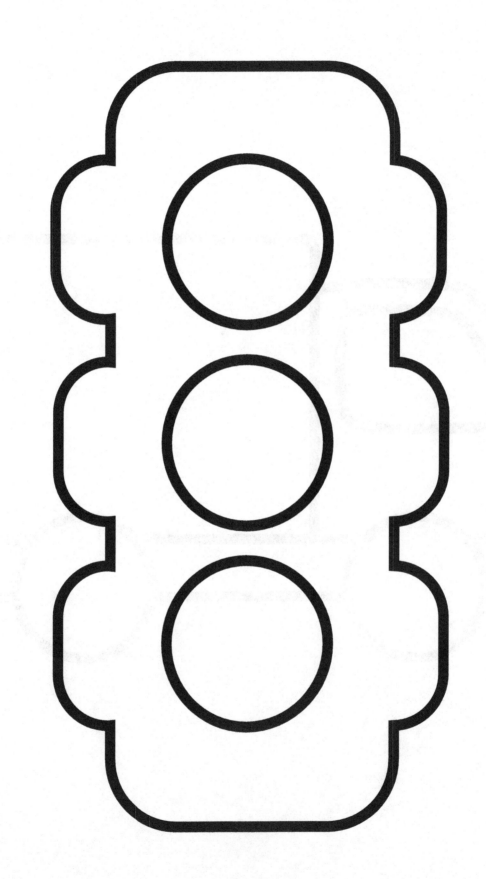

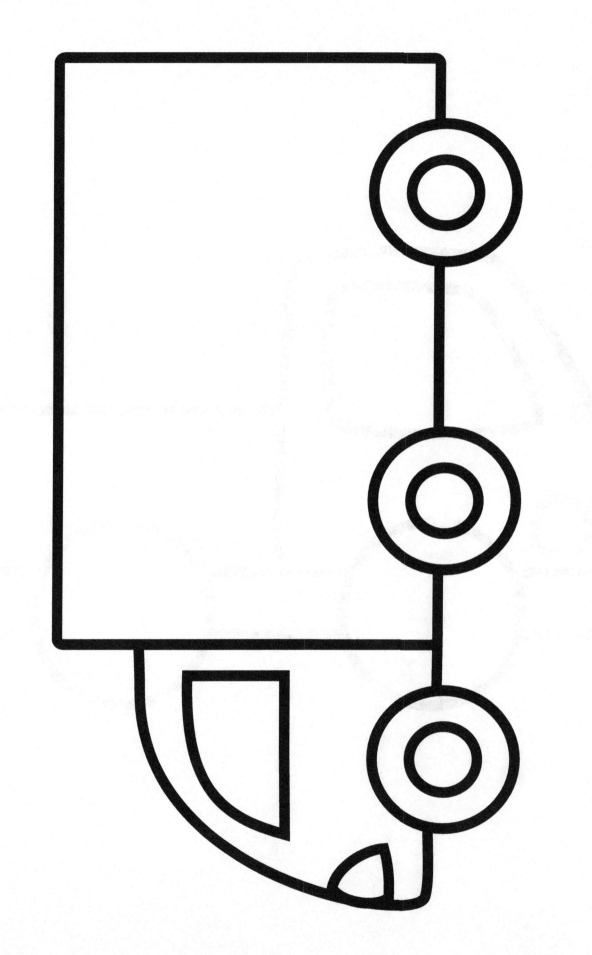

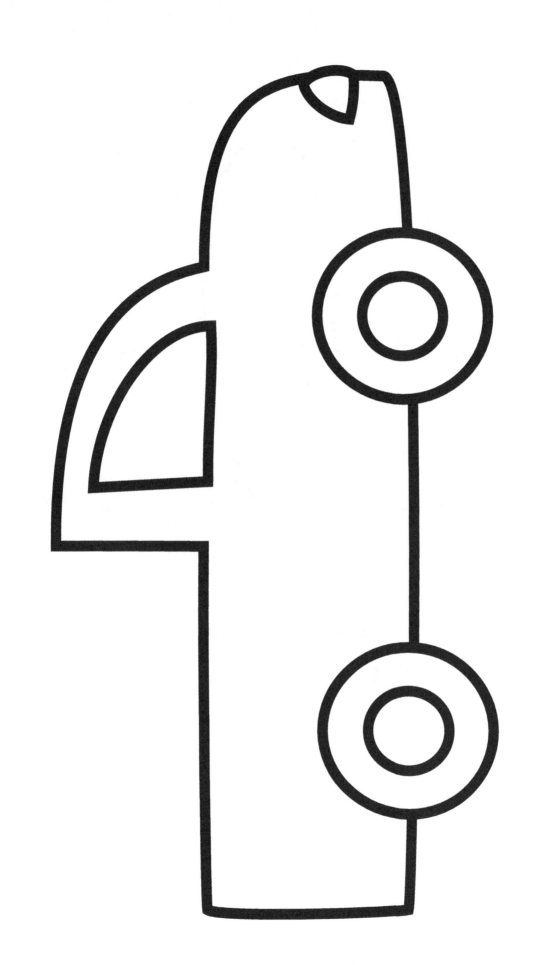

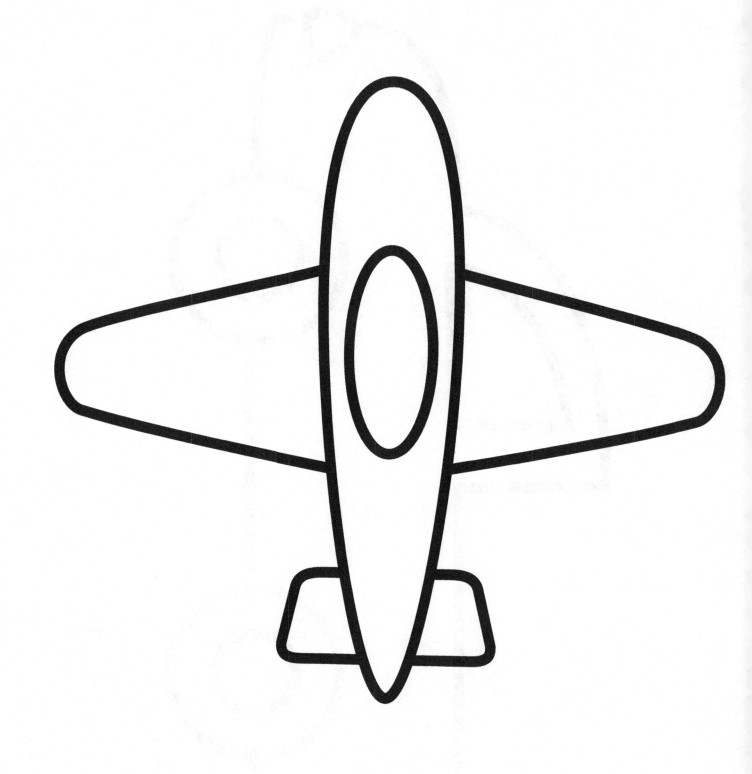

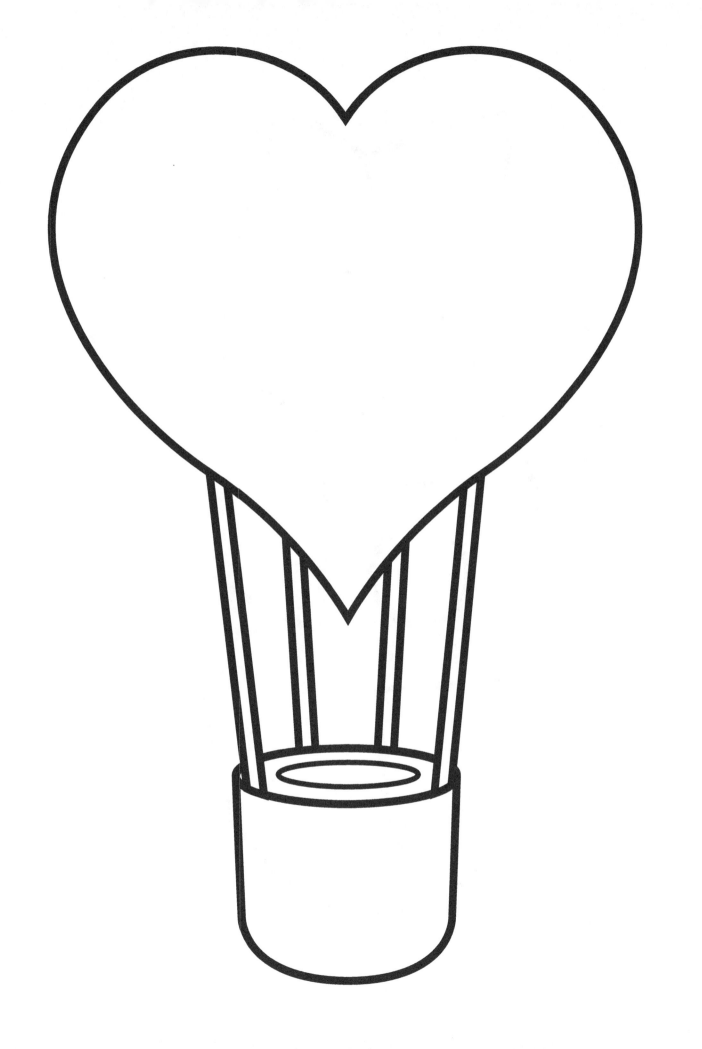

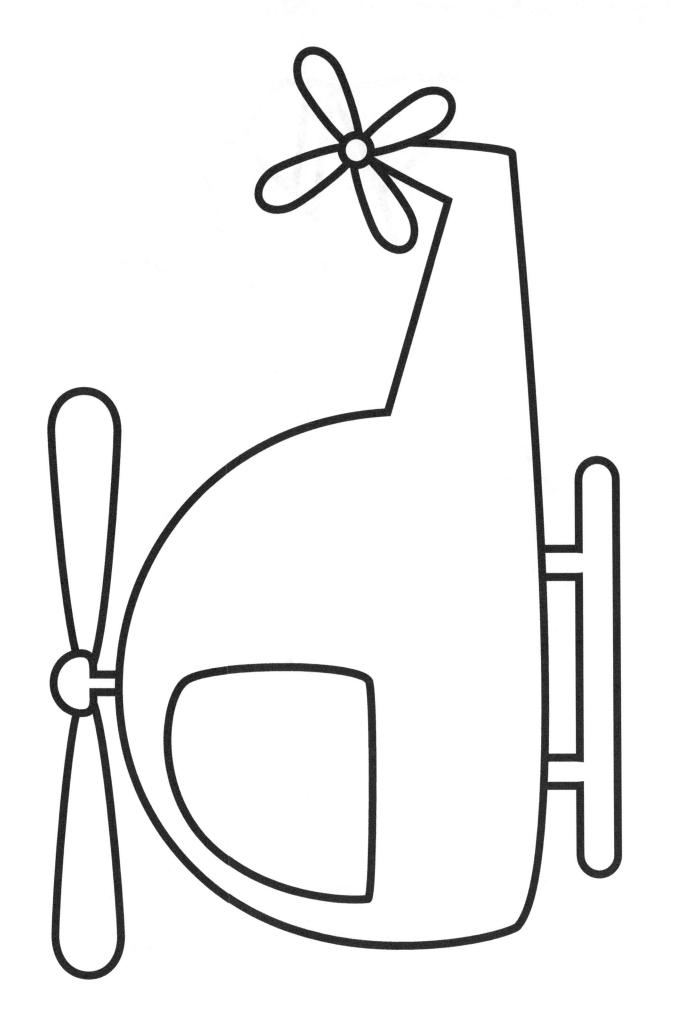

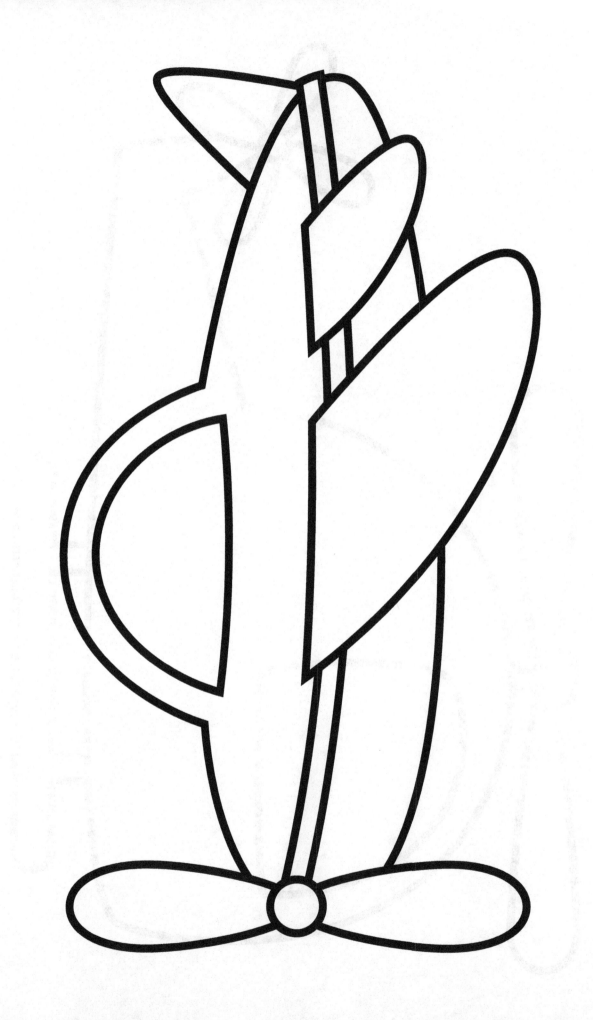

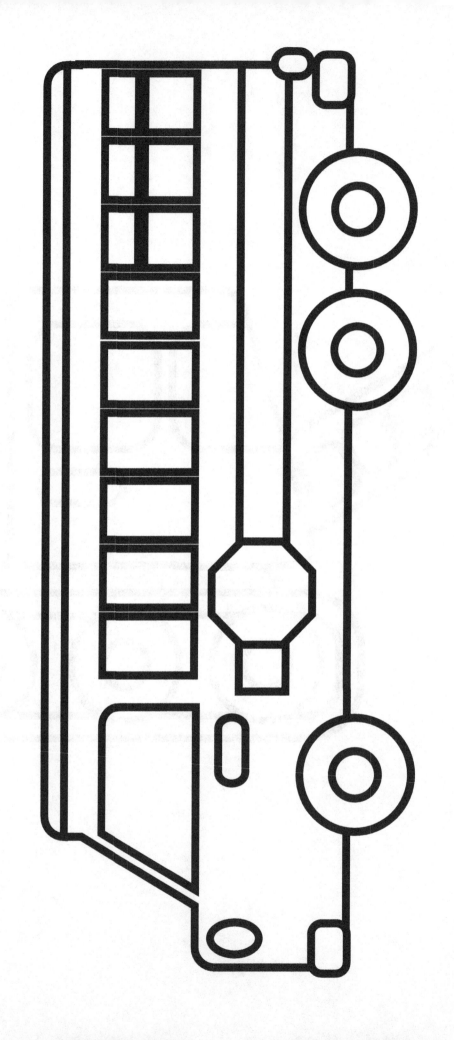

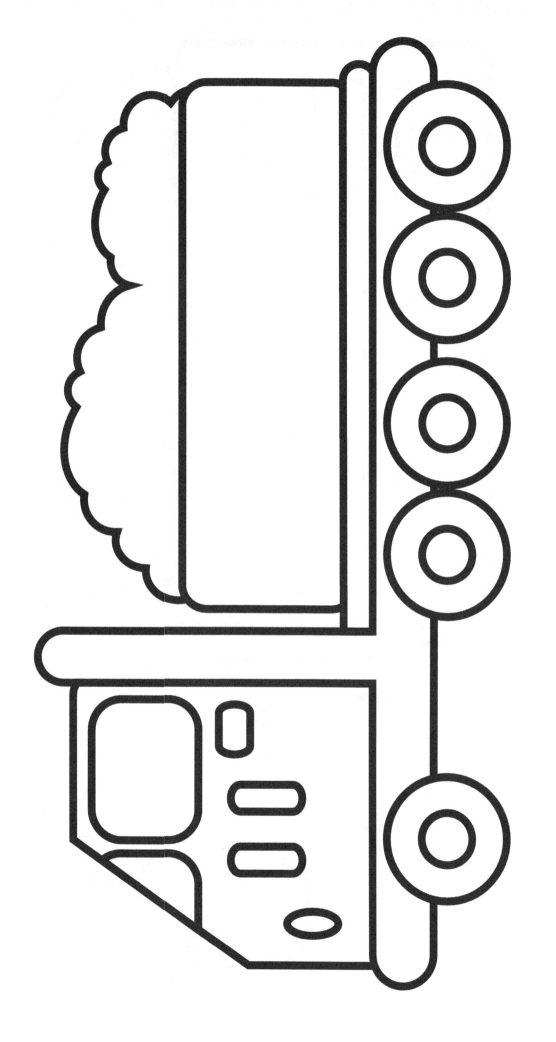

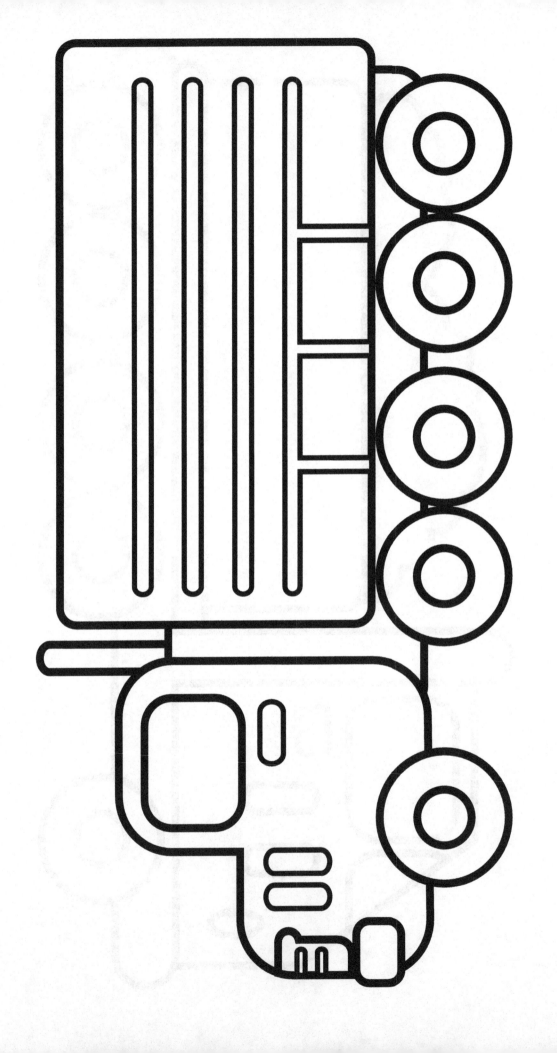

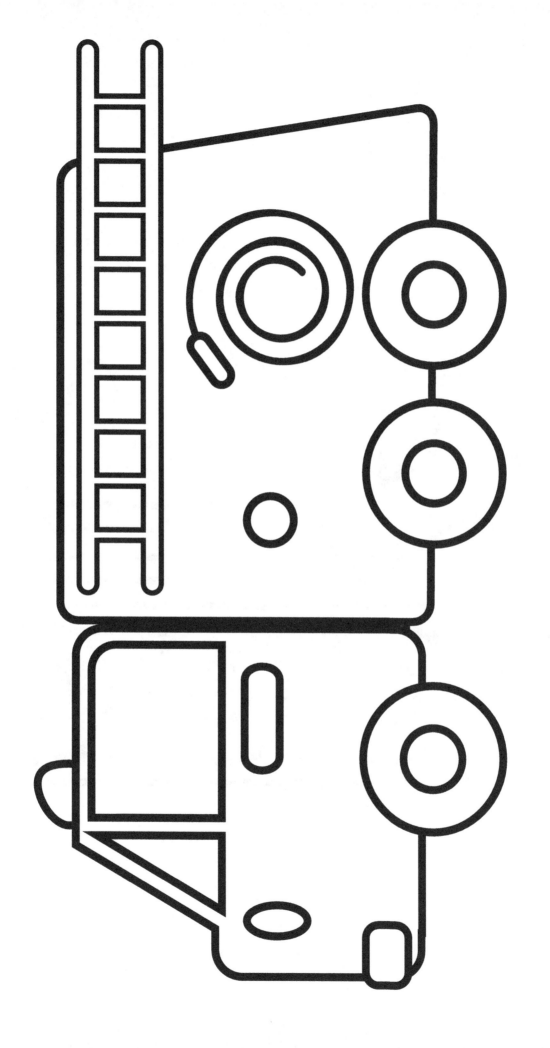

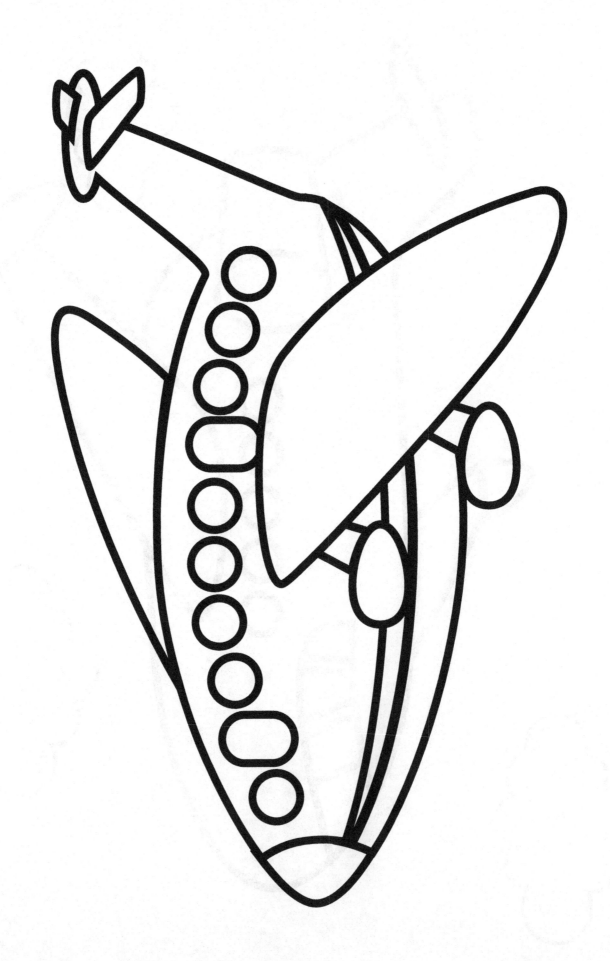

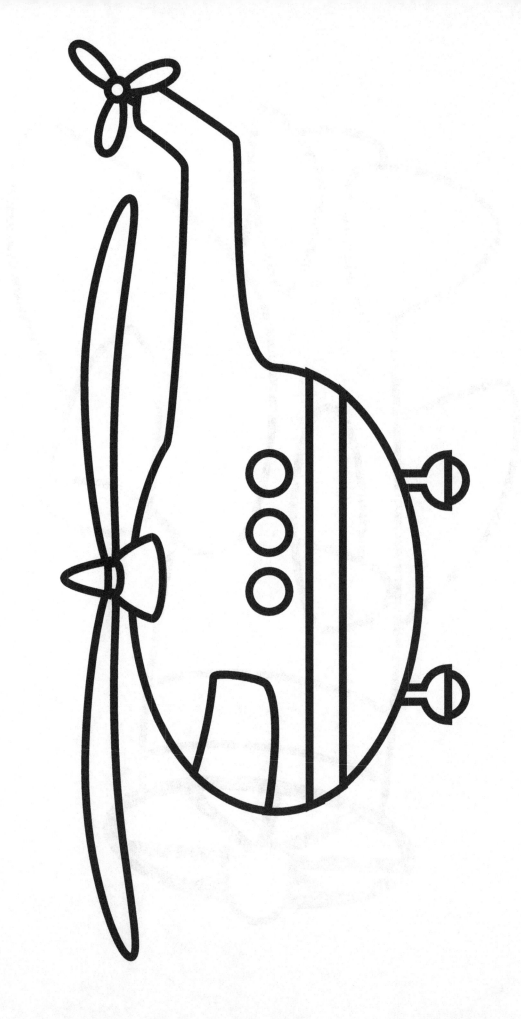

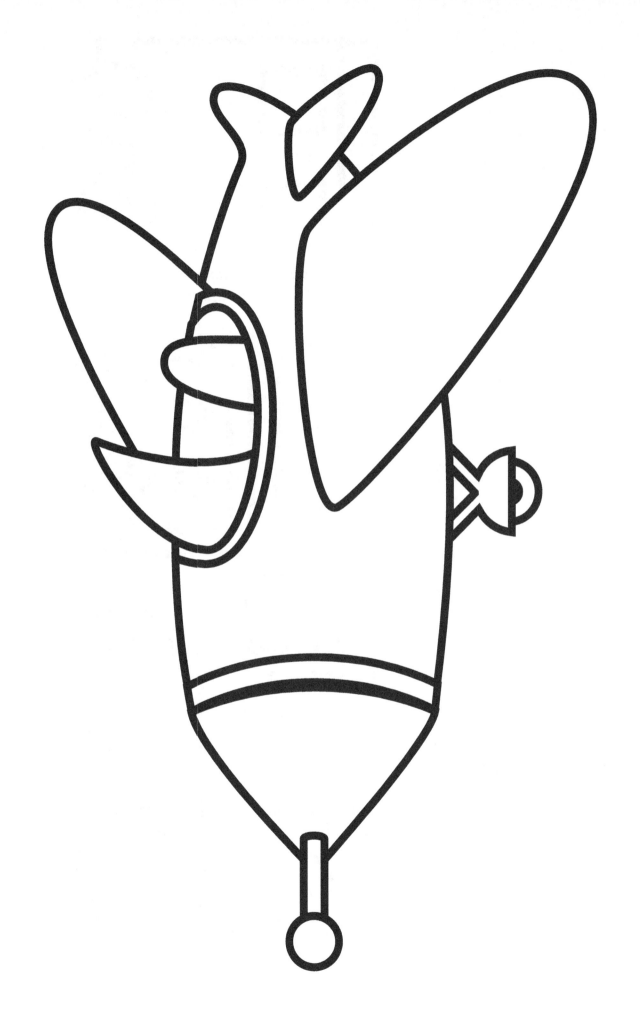

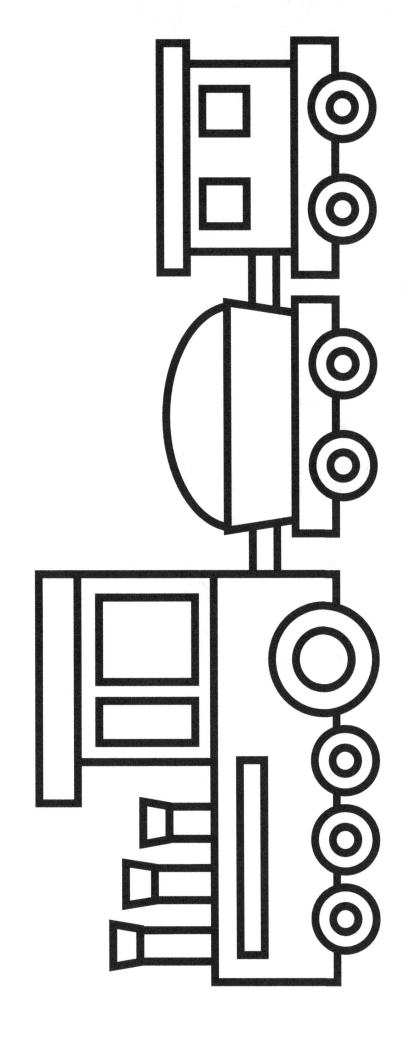

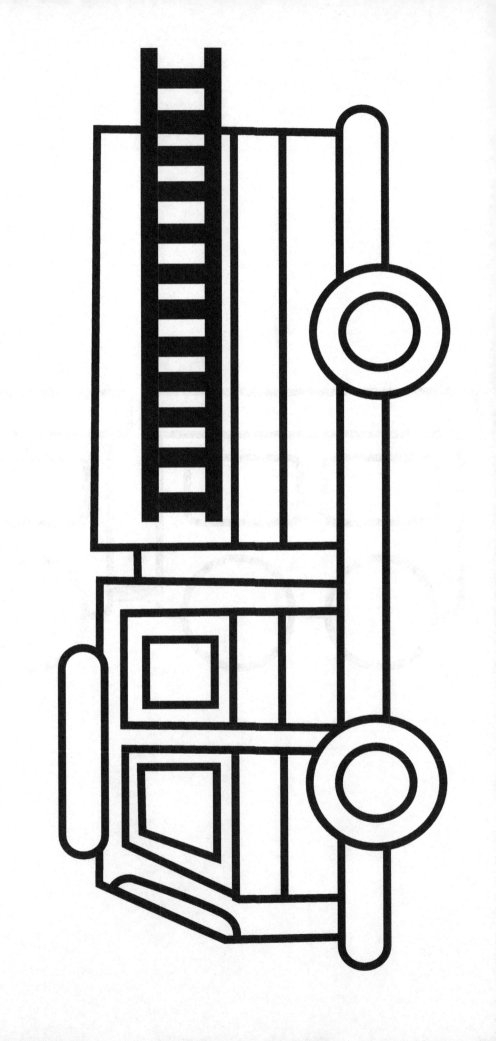

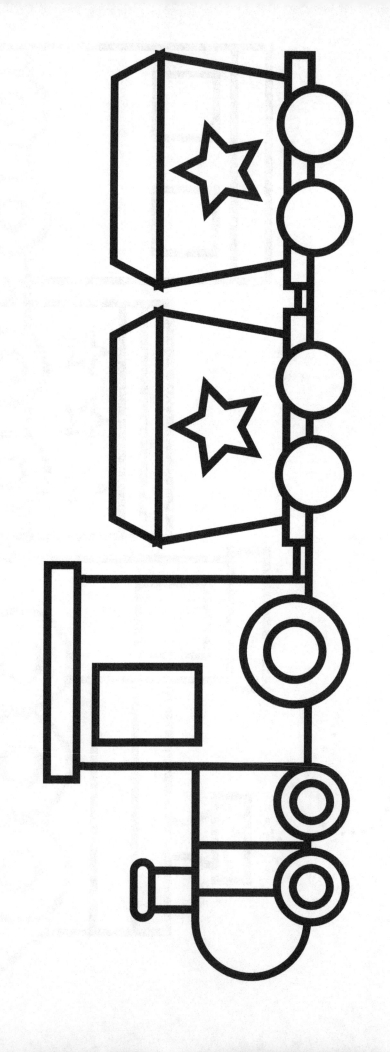

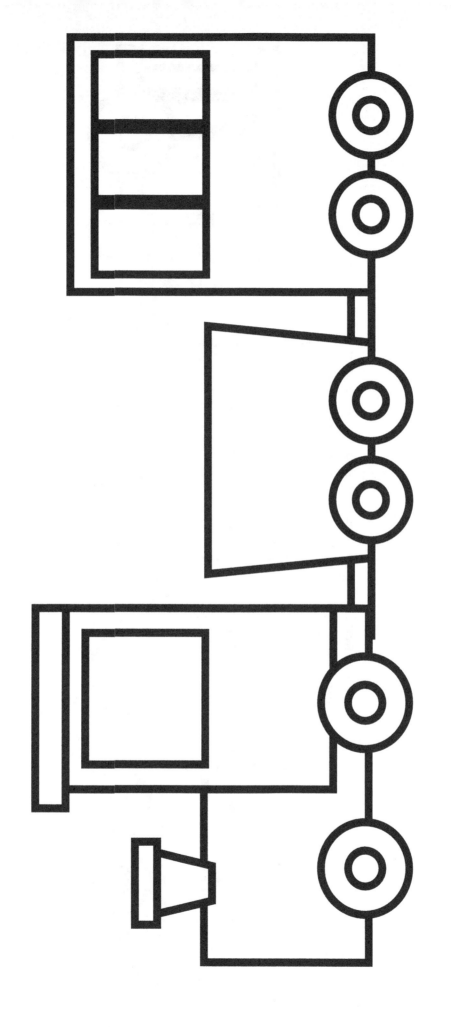

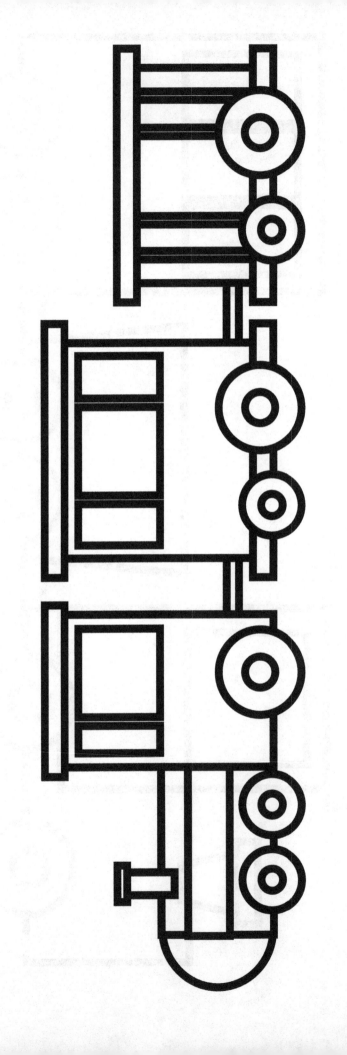

If you liked this coloring book...

Please leave us a 5 star review on Amazon, and check out other books by Elita Nathan.

Coloring Book for Kids: 100+ Coloring Pages, Hours of Fun: Animals, planes, trains, castles - coloring book for kids by Elita Nathan

- This coloring book is designed for young children and beginners. 100+ unique pictures, 100+ pages.
- Big simple pictures perfect for beginners
- Drawings designed so it's easy to stay inside the lines
- Thick outlines and large areas to color
- No movie or cartoon characters their own

Writing Prompts for Kids. Letter Tracing + Draw and Write Pages by Elita Nathan

- 50+ writing prompts appropriate for pre-K to 1st grade
- writing prompts that can be traced to practice handwriting
- suggested words to help your child complete the sentence
- large area for drawing to entice the little artists
- 50 blank pages without prompts for your child to write on their own

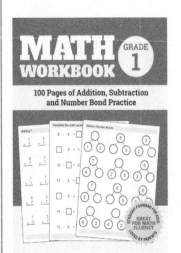

Math Workbook Grade 1: 100 Pages of Addition, Subtraction and Number Bond Practice by Elita Nathan

- We believe kids get better at math with practice, resulting in confidence and positive attitude towards math
- This workbook provides kids with additional math practice that reinforces and complements what is taught at school.
- There are no pictures or word problems, and focus on mastery of basic addition and subtraction.
- This workbook combines traditional addition and subtraction math problems, with number bond problems.

Congratulations!

is now a certified super coloring expert

Date

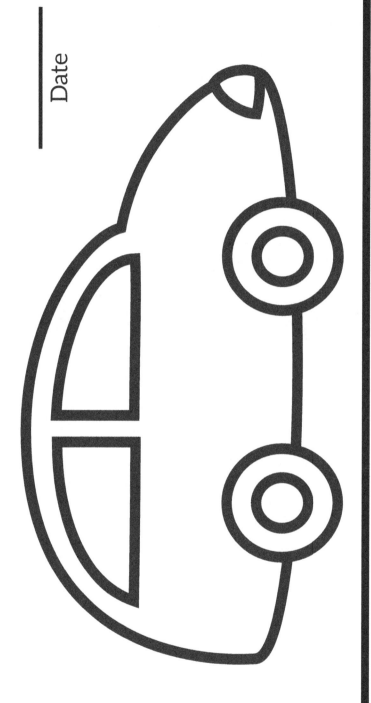

Made in the USA
Las Vegas, NV
16 September 2023

77684269R00063